by the same author
The Quantro Story (1978)
Double Mountain Crossing (1979)
The Fight at Hueco Tanks (1980)
The Copper City (1981)
Desperadoes (1981)

non-fiction
The History Of Saltburn (1983)

as editor
Cleveland Volume One (1984)

SALTBURN TIMES
Chris Scott Wilson

**seaside books
Saltburn**

First published by Seaside Books 1987
All Rights Reserved

© 1985/87 C.J.S. Wilson

ISBN: 0 9508631 3 0

LITHOGRAPHIC & LETTERPRESS PRINTERS

6 Amber Street, Saltburn-by-the-Sea, Cleveland. TS12 1DT.   Telephone: Guisborough (0287) 23756

Preface

When I began gathering material, a friend remarked "Are you doing a *Son of Saltburn?*" He was referring to my earlier publication *The History Of Saltburn*. When it was published my intention was to produce a companion volume of photographs, but only now has the opportunity arisen. Each of the books is designed to compliment the other.

I was extremely gratified by the reception given to the first book. Many people approached me with information and photographs. Thurston Printers unearthed a treasure trove of old printing blocks, inherited from the original owner of the business, Percy Thurston. Some of these grace the following pages. Perhaps most interesting were the people pleased to share their memories of the town in former days. It is hoped this book will provoke happy recollections of 'Saltburn Times'.

Saltburn-by-the-Sea 1986.

Acknowledgements

Most of the photographs and postcards in this book are from private collections. Without the co-operation of the people concerned, there would have been no book. Thanks are due to: Tommy Young (pages 40; 48; 51; 59; 65; 69;), Miss H. Metcalfe (pages 9; 37; 49; 53; 54; 57 left and centre; 61 top), Mrs. F. Woodrow-Brown (pages 12; 17; 19; 27; 32; 38; 44; 66; 70), Mr. and Mrs. A. Lynn (pages 11, 30; 33; 35; 43;), Thurston Printers pages 18; 20; 22; 34; 39; 46), Mrs. A. Mountain (page 21 top right), Michael Cummins (page 40), Bradley's Antiques and Country Pine (page 63) and Mrs. Grayson. My thanks also to Norman Bainbridge who copied cherished photographs, and also thanks to the many people who suggested avenues of exploration.

A Short History

The Saltburn best known today came into existence in the latter half of the 19th century. The town began on the clifftop and has since sprawled west and south with the addition of housing estates. The original hamlet of Saltburn faces the beach at sea level, and has dwindled from a population of some 87 people in 1841 to a handful. The homes of the villagers have slowly disappeared too, the Ship Inn expanding to swallow all the remaining row but for the last cottage toward Huntcliff. Behind Cat Nab one dwelling remains, but the rest are long demolished, vanished like the trades of their former occupants; sailors, dressmakers, millers, shoemakers, manservants, maidservants, paupers, not forgetting the preventative coastguards who were stationed at the specially built 'government buildings' above the Ship Inn.

The first human presence at Saltburn has been dated in the

Opposite: A copy of A. N. Carter's fanciful painting of Old Saltburn by Kathleen Ord. As well as tutoring pupils, Kathleen found time to produce many paintings and even personalised Christmas cards for Saltburn's residents. Her hand-painted postcards were on sale at the Spa for 1/- (5p).

Bronze Age, about 2300 BC. Excavations at Warsett Hill (which crowns Huntcliff) revealed bones and pottery buried in the centre of a stone circle, and bodies were also found in a well on the site of a Roman signal tower at the lip of the cliff. The watch tower was one of a chain built to warn the garrisons inland of attacks by Saxon pirates between 300-400 AD (the date confirmed by coins). It is likely a small community existed near the beach, probably in crude huts, scratching a living from the sea and supplying part of the legionaires' diet. When the centre of the Roman empire in the Mediterranean collapsed in the first decade of the 5th century, the legions were withdrawn from England. It appears, however, the Saxon pirates assaulted the outpost before the retreat, as the victims in the well had been beheaded.

Later in the same century, Angles, Saxons and Jutes flooded the country, spreading until they found suitable places to settle. Proof they approved of Saltburn was uncovered when an Anglian cemetery was disturbed on Hob Hill during mining operations in 1909. Almost 50 graves were discovered, revealing beads and brooches, knives and a throwing axe. Items were dated as from the 5th or 6th centuries.

After the Norman conquest in 1066, Saltburn became part of a barony dominated by a line of Norman Lords who occupied Skelton Castle, and in 1215 there was certainly a hermitage by the beck in the woods. This was given to the Abbey of Whitby by Roger de Argenton who held the manor of Upleatham. By 1464, the Conyers family ruled over Saltburn, Marske and

Opposite: Old Saltburn and Huntcliff in 1887 showing a wooden bridge spanning Skelton Beck in the foreground. Storms demolished a succession of these fragile structures.

Brotton when the Skelton estates were divided between three sisters. By that time the hamlet of Saltburn had developed, Fairfax-Blakeborough dating the Ship Inn from then, but in all likelihood not the same building. The locals were known for fishing and catching seals by dressing as women, but it was the mineral alum that was to boost trade.

In 1615 an alum works was opened at Selby Hagg, 1¼ miles inland from the coast. It would be Saltburn where the ships beached both to unload the urine necessary for the manufacturing process, and to load the finished product for shipment to the crown's London warehouse. By 1670 there were two alum mines actually sited at Saltburn, one on the east side of Skelton Beck, and the other on the west. They remained open until 1720. A brief revival occurred in 1765 but lasted only 11 years.

Saltburn's main trade for the next 50 years was smuggling. The hamlet became notorious for the luggers which sometimes moored in broad daylight to discharge illicit cargoes into willing hands. A government pamphlet published in 1779 claimed nearly 4 million gallons of geneva (gin) and almost 6 million pounds of tea were brought into England illegally each year. The onset of the French wars escalated the trade as commodities by regular routes became scarce. When in exile, Napoleon wrote that he ordered free access to the channel ports for English smugglers, while with the other hand he was fighting the English army and navy tooth and nail. The lugger captains were estimated to hand over £10,000 a week in hard gold for their cargoes, and Napoleon relied

on this coin to pay his troops.

Saltburn saw its share of goods, handled at the peak of the trade by a highly organised gang (see page 22). When cottages at the foot of Cat Nab were demolished about 1820, each was found to have a hidden cellar or false cupboard. However, when the battle of Waterloo successfully curtailed the French war, the English navy was run down and manpower resources were channelled into more effective policing of our shores. Saltburn was given its own detachment of coastguards housed in the row of cottages still seen on Huntcliff. Suppression took time, but by 1830 the local trade was all but extinct. Any revival was quashed in the 1840s when Sir Robert Peel spearheaded a movement for the abolition of duties on many of the previously highly profitable goods.

Saltburn reluctantly returned to being a sleepy fisher community, some of the men occupied seasonally in the collection of ironstone from the beach for shipping to Newcastle. Steady employment in this field was not secured until the first proper ironstone mine opened in 1864 at Hob Hill.

It was the 1850's before Henry Pease walked along the sandbanks from Marske and saw the hamlet of tumbledown cottages with a jumble of fishing boats drawn up in the lee of Huntcliff. Surprisingly, he looked instead at the opposite cliff where fields ran to the edge, and saw a town in his mind's eye. Henry Pease was a man of great conviction. He started things and saw them through to the end. He and his brother Joseph were both on the board of the Stockton and Darlington Railway, and like most

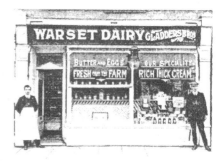

Above: Advertising circa 1918
Opposite: Looking toward the sea along Saltburn Gill. In the foreground is the flour mill, where a contraband stowhole was found near the grinding wheel during demolition about 1905.

businessmen, knew the secret of success was to expand and diversify. Moreover, if one project could support another, then both had a better chance of survival.

The Pease family originated in Darlington, their wealth generated by wool mills. Henry's brother Joseph had conceived the idea of a port at the mouth of the Tees as an adjunct to Darlington. Coal could be shipped from the South Durham collieries, thus stealing Stockton's trade. He formed the Owners of The Middlesbrough Estates to buy land for resale to developers, who came in plenty when Middlesbrough began to expand after John Vaughan's discovery of iron ore in the Cleveland Hills. With their railway pushing into East Cleveland where mining surveyors were running amok, eager to secure mineral rights, Henry's idea of developing Saltburn only differed from Joseph's inasmuch as he saw Saltburn as a holiday resort rather than a working town.

If ironstone mining in East Cleveland proved fruitless, then the railway would not have been wasted. It has been written Henry's vision was of a *'white celestial city'*. It must be remembered that the white firebrick stipulated for building would come from Pease West brickworks in County Durham, another way of ensuring a return on investment. Strangely enough, years later Alfred Pease was to remark that if his grandfather Joseph had not been nearly blind he would have discouraged the use of white firebrick as it gave the town such a cold appearance.

From the beginning it was decided Saltburn was to be upmarket. Ironmasters, whose works were springing up along the

Right: Henry Pease, Saltburn's main founder.
Far Right: Henry's brother Joseph, founder of Middlesbrough.

Opposite: A celebration in Station Square, perhaps lifeboat day. Hard work for one horse!

Tees could buy villas where their families could spend the summers while the ironmasters themselves were still close to the office. Although the common working men did not yet have paid holidays, subsidised railfares could tempt them to visit the resort for the day with their families, providing turnover for local shopkeepers, but more importantly for the Stockton and Darlington Railway. While the Zetland Hotel could cater to wealthy visitors, the streets behind the seafront could house the sector employed in service industries, and also provide lodging houses for those among the middle class who could afford moderate seaside holidays. With these ideas in mind, Henry Pease formed the Saltburn Improvement Company in 1859, and the following year approached Lord Zetland in order to buy 10 acres of land on the cliff top. Within 16 years the company would purchase a total of 135 acres. The contract for designing the new town was won by George Dickenson, and by 1861 the first streets were being laid out. The Stockton and Darlington railway tracks were creeping along the coast and tenders had been invited for the building of the Zetland Hotel. The next 10 years saw Saltburn By The Sea rise where previously had been ploughed fields. Although the town never really expanded at a rate to fully satisfy Henry Pease and the board of the Improvement Company, it gathered popularity as more amenities were introduced. The Valley Gardens (then known as the Pleasure Grounds), the pier and the later the cliff railway, and the graceful span of the Ha'penny bridge all added to Saltburn's charm, but perhaps its greatest attraction for

Queen Hotel

ordinary folk was the opportunity to see first hand how the rich lived, riding in fine carriages and attended by clutches of liveried servants. It was this image Saltburn's Improvement Committee, and subsequently the District Councils, fought to preserve.

By 1910, almost 30 years after Henry Pease's death, most of the gaps in the town had been filled in. The seafront facade was as complete as it would ever be and both sides of the main shopping centre, Station Street, had been built. The private housing sector had begun its crawl west toward Marske. The period immediately prior to World War I was probably when Saltburn's popularity was at its height. Railway stations all over the country boasted posters proclaiming Saltburn's delights. Pierrots performed on pitches throughout the town while bands played on the pier and in the Valley Gardens. Visitors could bathe in the sea or luxuriate in the brine baths, and even see their names printed in the columns of two Saltburn newspapers. Stars of the motor racing world could be watched wrestling with the steering wheels of powerful automobiles during the annual Open Speed Trials, racing to Marske and back. Dances were held at the Spa Assembly Rooms between theatrical productions, and the boatmen pulled visitors round the bay, regaling them with exciting stories of shipwrecks or lurid tales of the running fights between the King's Riding Officers and the smugglers who frequented the Ship Inn.

Between the wars Saltburn was still a regular call for day-trippers and holidaymakers, but after World War II the pierrots no longer had pitches on the sands. The Open Speed Trials had

Above: Letterhead block in use today. Opposite: The motor bike in the centre of Station Street dates this photograph about 1920.

been transferred to Redcar because of beach deterioration. In the 1950's when the cars grew too fast for adequate safety precautions, the races were finally abandoned. But the fifties did bring a housing boom to Saltburn, estates completed along Marske Road, the last being Wilton Bank in the 1970s.

Landmarks disappeared in the old town. John Anderson's hotel, The Alexandra, closed in 1973 to become the Edward and Alexandra luxury apartments. In 1974 a severe storm carried away the pierhead and only a few months later the prohibitive cost of maintenance resulted in the demolition of the Ha'penny Bridge. In Station Square the brine baths, long closed, were finally sold and reduced to rubble in 1976.

Although Saltburn still attracts a crop of summer tourists, and is probably far larger than Henry Pease ever imagined, the town really serves as home to many daily commuters to Teesside whose livings are earned in industry and commerce. Once when I replied to a query with the answer 'I live in Saltburn', my questioner said *'Oh, you mean where the five bob snobs live?'*

Saltburn still has a reputation after all.

Below right: Letterpress block of Huntcliff.
Right: E. A. Whipham, c1885, Agent for Saltburn Improvement Company & The Owners of The Middlesbrough Estates.
Far Right: Hansom cabs in Station Square from a postcard dated 1914. The buildings on the right were bombed in World War II, later replaced by a glass showroom.

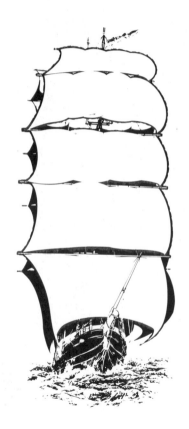

The Ship Inn

Once upon a time the hamlet of Saltburn is said to have sported four inns. They carried names like The Nimrod, The Seagull and The Dolphin, but the only survivor is The Ship Inn. In its four or five hundred years it has been enlarged, the original bar closest to the road. Apart from the locals, regular customers were hunters on trips to shoot cormorants along Huntcliff. Previous callers had been the press gangs, scouring the coast for likely men to crew His Majesty's ships. The Preventative men too, often searched the tavern. But the softest footfalls were surely those of the smugglers who haunted the Ship Inn.

At one time it was estimated the majority of villagers along the North East coast of Yorkshire earned their crusts by running contraband. Tea, coffee, chocolate, lace and silk all came ashore, but more importantly what were regarded as the staples of life-

An undated painting by Albert Strange.

Opposite: Cottages by the Ship Inn, fallen into disrepair.

tobacco, wine, brandy and geneva (gin - that most English of liquors). While a gallon of gin cost about £1, Customs duty was 6d (2½p) and Excise duty 5/- (25)p. Temptation was too great to resist.

The Ship's most famous landlord was undoubtedly John Andrew, a Scot born in 1761 who came to make his home in Yorkshire and take a wife. It is likely Saltburn was already a 'runners' route ashore when he became landlord in 1780/81, but it was Andrew's organisational flair which crafted an efficient team which dominated local trade. His partner was Thomas King of Kirkleatham, a brewer. Supplying most of the local gentry proved so lucrative they invested in their own lugger, *The Morgan Rattler*, cutting out the middle man. *Rattler's* commander, Captain Brown, was said to be cut of a fierce jib, his wicked grin supported by a pair of matched pistols stuck close to hand in his belt.

John Andrew was the man to handle such a mariner. Even in later life Andrew was still of imposing presence and always ready to fight for his right as a free trader. There are many stories of running skirmishes between the prevenatives and the smugglers, mostly legend. One such is that Andrew's men were surrounded on the beach at Saltburn one night in 1810 by a Riding Officer and dragoons. Simultaneously, a revenue cutter swept round Huntcliff to capture the lugger. Andrew was watching and quickly sent for reinforcements who beat off the King's men, while offshore the lugger sheared her anchor and fled. While the Customs cutter used a few pounds of powder and shot

Above. The signature of the smuggler John Andrew on the first roll of the Roxby & Cleveland Hounds.
Opposite: A fairly early postcard.

firing chasers, the lugger gained her freedom with only a few scars.

The risks paid high dividends. Wealthy, John Andrew moved up to the White House overlooking Saltburn Glen. The Ship was still used as a way station and reputedly a tunnel linked it to the White House. In 1966 workmen laying drains at the Ship found a tunnel, but it was earlier claimed this was merely a stowhole into the cliff, walled up in 1882.

John Andrew was also an instigator and founder member of the Cleveland Hounds, surviving today as the Cleveland Hunt. As President and Master of Fox Hounds, the hunt was based at the White House, completing his facade as a wealthy land owner. He still persisted with his smuggling activities, notching up a record of close brushes with the King's men until he was caught red-handed at Hornsea in 1827, arrested and jailed in York Castle. It is said he even directed his illegal affairs from behind bars. Two years later he was released and returned home, dogged by ill health until his death on 14 November 1835.

The Ship Inn moved out of the Andrew family's hands. A later landlord also to get his name in the papers was William Temple. He tried to commit suicide by swallowing rat poison, but prompt action saved his life.

Improvements to the Ship Inn came slowly. Electricity for private consumption was introduced to Saltburn in 1900, but hurricane-style lamps were still being used in the inn as late as World War II. Today the Ship is at least three times larger than during those smuggling days, and is ever popular with summer visitors. Standing in the doorway late at night, it is easy to imagine the twinkling lights of a ship in the bay are the lanterns of a lugger, eager hands stealthily lowering casks of geneva into cobles for the run ashore . . .

Right: Cows were periodically allowed onto the beach where licking the mineral-rich seaweed supplemented their diet.
Opposite: Cat Nab and Old Saltburn looking toward the sea. The farm on the left was known as Dove's or Flintoff's. On many photographs the lean-to "threepenny-bit" style open sided barn is not evident.

Cat-Nab.

The Zetland Hotel

One of Saltburn's most prominent features, the Zetland Hotel, was visualised and planned to be just that. If the Stockton and Darlington Railway Co. built the Zetland on a lavish scale, then it would attract a wealthy class of customer. The shareholders of the Saltburn Improvement Company were fully aware a side effect would be easier seduction of other developers who would view the railway's investment as a show of confidence in the new town. The Stockton and Darlington Railway had provisionally budgeted £8,000 for the new hotel only after infighting among board members, some of whom thought it madness. But by February 1861 a fee was offered for the best design, and by July the plans were on show at the company's office in Darlington. Contractors were asked to submit tenders before the closing date of 25th July. The winning architect was William Peachy of

The Zetland Hotel. Note the vacant plot at the foot of Milton Street.

Above: The Wesleyan Methodist Church on Milton Street opened 1865 Opposite: The staff of the Zetland Hotel in 1887. The Manager, Mr. Verini, can be seen in the centre.

Darlington, whose visits to the site obviously impressed him as he later bought property in Saltburn. The town also provided him with commissions. As well as the prestigious Zetland, he designed the Wesleyan Chapel in Milton Street and the post office in Station Street.

Contracts were quickly signed, the hotel's foundation stone laid by Lord Zetland on 2nd October 1861. The stables at the rear appear to have been completed first. Prior to having their own place of worship, the Wesleyan Methodists used the hayloft to hold services before moving on to the railway station waiting room.

Lord Zetland returned to Saltburn to perform the Hotel's opening ceremony on 27 July 1863. No expense had been spared. George Tweddell in his *Visitors' handbook* (1863) writes of the hotel as *'a princely pile . . . in the Italian style of architecture . . . of firebricks, and the front is 60 yards in length . . . The front and sides have spacious terraces, with perforated balustrades of terra-cotta, surmounted with vases of flowers: and a neat balcony runs along the whole front of the middle storey. A semi-circular tower rises in the centre of the front, which is used as a telescope room, and is provided with another balcony; and both from the top of this tower and from the balcony the view is gorgeous. The hotel contains about 90 rooms, comprising about 50 bedrooms, a large dining and coffee room, a ladies' coffee and drawing room, reading room, smoking room, billiard room etc.'*

Although the writer says: *'The fitting-up is all in a style of palatial dignity, and nothing is left short which can add to the comfort of the*

Above: Old printer's block.
Opposite: The Zetland Hotel Stables, showing carriages for hire.

guests,' contemporary photographs reveal the interior to be spartan by today's standards, but similar to country houses of the period. The bill for making affluent guests feel at home exceeded preliminary costings. Estimates vary from the stated budget of £8,000 up to £40,000.

When the railway company advertised for a manager, the prospective employee was to propose his/her own salary, and would also receive a bonus of 5% of the net profit generated above a predetermined level.

As well as recreational rooms mentioned, the hotel boasted lawn tennis courts facing Dundas Street (now a car park), and the hire of *'every description of conveyance including bath chairs'*. Also offered were hot and cold sea and fresh water baths, while the hotel's stables would provide salt water, 3 gallons for 1d (½p).

The special railway platform was another luxury. After running into Saltburn station, the main line continued to within a few yards of the hotel's rear door. This was covered by a roof to shield arrivals should the weather be inclement.

The hotel proved popular. In 1876 magistrates granted an extension of opening hours from 10pm to 11pm to encourage trade. Alcoholic drinks, however, were still not allowed for consumption on the open terraces. In August 1882 John Richardson was summonsed for drinking a glass of beer outside the hotel. His excuse of *'having an open-air supper'* failed to convince the justices who fined him 5/- (25)p, while the Zetland's manager, Mr Verini, paid a 5/- fine for supplying him.

The Alexandra Hotel & Saltburn Pier

Almost a mandatory adornment of Victorian seaside reorts was a pier, presumably to provide the illusion of taking a voyage without undergoing discomfort or the possible rigours of sea-sickness. Saltburn was no exception. Any idea that could attract more visitors was always supported wholeheartedly by the business community. In 1861 the newly born Saltburn Improvement Company was keeping a watchful eye on the labourers constructing Alpha Place in preparation for the railway's arrival. Tenders had been invited for the station and the Zetland Hotel, both intended as showpieces to form the nucleus of the new town. A bridge across the Glen had been proposed, and also a pier, but as all available capital was committed, the discussion was postponed.

The man to fan the idea back into flame was John Anderson,

Saltburn, View from the Pier.

owner of an inventive mind and the perseverance to see his schemes fulfilled. He was a railway engineer who had worked with the Stockton and Darlington, and the South Durham and Lancashire Union railways. In Saltburn he saw the opportunity of making an investment which would pay future dividends. When the groundplan was drawn for the town he immediately bought plots of land in Milton and Amber Streets, but his most important acquisition was the site on Britannia Terrace/Marine Drive (both now Marine Parade) where he planned to build a hotel. That he was closely linked with the Improvement Company is evident as he was the only hotelier to be granted a liquor license by the Improvement Committee (beside the Zetland Hotel). Prior to the Local Board or District Council, this committee approved uses for all buildings. They were determined to project a 'genteel' image as opposed to the Blackpool-type resorts.

The Alexandra Hotel, complete with 100 rooms, opened in 1867 and became known by the locals as simply Anderson's Hotel. By this time he had been retained as resident engineer for the Improvement Company. The Alexandra was barely open when a meeting was held there to discuss a pier. No doubt goaded by

Opposite: A contemporary drawing of the Alexandra Hotel and Britannia Terrace from a souvenir booklet.
Below: A printer's block commissioned for the hotel, probably for a bill header or letterhead.

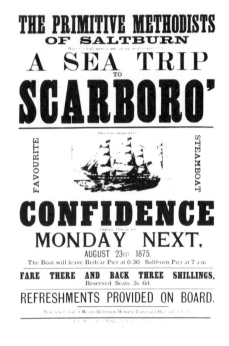

Above: A reproduction poster, given away by the even quality of the typeface.

the knowledge Redcar had decided the previous year to build a pier, Anderson had already given the matter serious thought. Not only had he drawn plans and selected materials, he had prepared costings. As Redcar's pier was to be 1200 feet, Anderson proposed Saltburn's should be 1500 feet. It would have 6 shops near the centre and a grand saloon at the head. He estimated a cost of £6,000 against Redcar's £10,000.

Anderson's presentation was so impressive, the proposal to launch the Saltburn-By-The-Sea Pier Company Ltd. with provisional share captial of £7,500 was met with immediate pledges of £2,000. The contract for iron work went to Cochrane & Grove's Ormesby Foundry and castings had already arrived when high construction tenders induced the directors to ask Anderson to act as contractor as well as engineer. He agreed.

On 26 January 1868 the first pile was driven by Mrs Thomas Vaughan of Gunnergate Hall and by May 1869 the pier was open. Over 50,000 people trod the boards within the first six months, the project an initial success. The first improvement was a vertical hoist, designed by Anderson, and built of timber secured by guylines. A circular cage held 20 people, raised and lowered by a counter-balance water tank. At the end of the pier was a landing stage where coastal steamers called to pick up passengers for Scarborough and Bridlington. By 1873 it was decided to add the 'grand saloon' earlier promised, and also to install gas lighting the length of the pier. A poor season necessitated raising extra capital for these improvements, and unfortunately gales and

41

Previous page: The vertical hoist and pier shortly after opening. Note bathing machines seen through the timberwork, and also octagonal payboxes.

Opposite: A later view in 1887 after the pierhead had been enlarged with payboxes now rectangular.

Inset: The new pierhead with glass screens.

heavy seas two years later on 15 October 1875 washed away the pierhead and landing stage. Almost bankrupt, the Pier Co was forced to reduce the length to 1250 feet and simplify the landing point.

By 1879 the annual profit was barely enough to cover interest on outstanding loans. The directors decided to liquidate. After long meetings, longer silences and few offers, the Pier Co sold out to The Owners Of The Middlesbrough Estates in August of 1883. Meanwhile, the hoist and pier had been inspected, repairs needed to the tune of £4,000. By June 1884 the pierhead had been enlarged, *'prettily designed windscreens'* added. It appears the original octagonal payboxes were replaced by square ones at this time.

The new owners concluded the vertical hoist had seen its best days, still functional but occasionally erratic. They replaced it with a more serviceable inclined tramway, opened in June 1884, worked by the same principle of counterbalancing water tanks. Far more durable than the hoist, the tramway is still one of Saltburn's attractions. There has never been an accident, the closest incident occurring when a small child strayed onto the track and was rescued by Jack Grapho, a pierrot. Instrumental in saving a life also was the pier. Before World War 1 Herbert Samuel, MP for Cleveland, was in difficulty during a morning swim. He was seen from the pier, two boatmen putting off to rescue him. But drowning was not the only danger Saltburn's waters held. On 31st August 1899 a woman on the pier spotted

a shark swimming nearby. Having seen such things in the Indian Ocean, she called to a boatman who succeeded in gaffing the shark which was later displayed on the beach.

One great enemy to piers is shipping. Although steamers had proved more dependable against the ill temper of the world's oceans, and were drastically reducing the number of shipwrecks, many sailing ships still plied the trade routes. The *Ovenbeg*, carrying china clay from Cornwall to Grangemouth was driven ashore at Saltburn on 7 May 1924 to the west of the pier. Hopes of refloating her faded as the heavily running sea and shrieking wind left her butting the pier like an angry bull. The pier decking

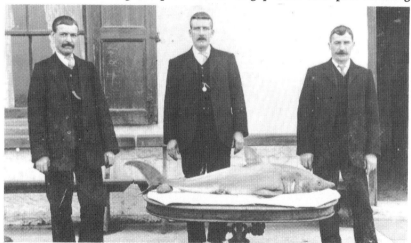

Right: Unknown fishermen outside the Ship Inn showing off a porbeagle shark, which may be the one mentioned in the text.
Opposite: One of Raphael Tuck & Sons "Framed Gem Glosso" postcards circa 1900, printed in Saxony. Note number of cottages beyond Ship Inn.

and piles were prised apart, *Ovenbeg* ploughing through to leave a 64 metre gap before she broke up on the beach near the foot of Saltburn Bank.

The pierhead remained an island until the 1930's when the breach was respanned and a small theatre was added between the entrance pay boxes. Concert parties were staged for the visitor's entertainment. The Council has persisted since formation to acquire Saltburn's amenities. In 1938 they bought the pier, then watched the Royal Engineers dismantle the rebuilt section to prevent possible use as a landing ramp should the Germans choose Saltburn for a beach-head. Only by the 1950s was the pier again complete and open, but damage occurred again in 1953 after storm conditions.

Surprisingly, it appears the pier was more popular this century than last. While the two companies who previously operated it always struggled to cover costs, in the long run the council have managed to make a profit. Between 1969-74 while maintenance cost £12,000, income was £20,000. During 1973 however a major overhaul was necessary. Unfortunately, before work could be completed, a violent storm on 29th October 1974 tore away the head and the pilings back to where *Ovenbeg* breached in 1924. The next day scavengers collected most of the timber before council workmen arrived. I have it on authority one man gathered enough of the decking to build a complete garden shed!

After much discussion on its future, a small pierhead was built on the much shortened structure, and entrance fees were waived.

Above: Letterhead block.
Right: An unkown soldier in front of a photographer's painted backdrop of Saltburn.
Far Right: A postcard of the Church of Emmanuel mailed 28th March 1905, using a ½d stamp.

Above: The entrance from Riftswood into the Pleasure Grounds. The head gardener's cottage was later superceded by the bungalow seen today. Opposite: Marske Mill Farm. The mill building is shown on the left.

Riftswood & Marske Mill

Before the establishment of Saltburn Parish in 1873, all land west of Skelton Beck in the woods lay in the parish of Marske (the hamlet of Saltburn being in the chapelry of Brotton). Thus the farm which stood on the flat section of land near the beck (now in the shadow of the viaduct) was known as Marske Mill, Marske's farmers hauling their grain there for grinding into flour. Hence also Marske Mill Lane, which leads to the farm.

In ancient times mills were often the property of the Lord of the Manor, and leased to to the miller. Certainly Lord Zetland operated this arrangement with Marske Mill during the 1800s. There is no indication of how long the farm had stood there, although the house shown in photographs appears to be Victorian, but perhaps this replaced an earlier building.

The farm was always noted for illness. Mist definitely lays

Saltburn, Riftswood Mill.

HUGH COATES,
Boot & Shoe Maker,
1, DUNDAS STREET (Near the Zetland Hotel)
Saltburn-by-the-Sea.

A good assortment of Ladies', Gents', and Children's Boots and Shoes in stock.

REPAIRS NEATLY AND PROMPTLY EXECUTED.

Sole Agent for the "K" Boot.

Opposite: A view from the farmyard to the railway viaduct erected 1871/2 In the right foreground the millrace can be seen.

longer in that part of Riftswood than in the rest of town. In January 1885 the beckwater also contributed to a typhoid outbreak at the mill. At first it was thought the drinking well was to blame. The Local Board of Health ordered it sealed, but by April it was realised the beck was responsible, contaminated by sewage from Skelton. Arguments between the two local boards continued for some years, Saltburn actually taking the Skelton & Brotton Board to court in 1894. After all the paper shuffling and shouting the problem was eventually resolved.

Because the farm had become part of Saltburn parish it was decided in 1900 that it should have a name change to Rifts Glen Mill as the town already had a flour mill behind Cat Nab. On postcards it was called Riftswood Mill, but of course to the locals it always remained Marske Mill. The path through the woods to and from Skelton was well used, and during the early part of this century the farmer's wife served teas and refreshments outside. (Note the tables on the right of the photograph on the previous page).

The mill farm has disappeared, demolished after years of disuse, but evidence of the foundations can still be seen, as can the dam whose purpose was to concentrate water flow to turn the mill wheel. Strangely, the farm's outline is still on Ordnance Survey maps. In recent years the builders Page-Johnson sought and were granted planning permission to develop a 24 unit executive housing project near the bottom of the lane, just above the mill site. Only after strenuous opposition by the Parish Council was the plan abandoned.

Saltburn Viaduct

The Valley Gardens

When Henry Pease first considered Saltburn for development, one of the natural features he was sure could be turned to advantage was the Glen running inland from the beach toward Skelton. He saw it as an integral part of the new resort. After his death, Henry's wife was to write that Saltburn's gardens had been his chief delight.

The appeal of gardens open to the public may seem strange in today's context. It must be remembered that most of the working population at that time toiled seven days a week, especially when employed in heavy industry. Their homes were necessarily close to workplaces because of the lack of an adequate public transport system. For town-bred children, the grimy streets were their playground. Saltburn must have seemed a magical place to them, golden sands curving under Huntcliff, a pier jutting out into the

Opposite: A late postcard of the north entrance to the gardens showing the span of the Ha'penny Bridge and the miniature railway opened in 1947. On the right can be seen the old turnstile for "receipt of custom".

North Sea and the bonus of woods and gardens to wander through without fear of over-zealous gamekeepers. Just to picnic on the grass in fresh air must have been novel, a welcome escape from living under a sky into which Teesside's numerous open-topped blast furnaces belched fire and smoke twenty-four hours a day. There was no soot on Saltburn's buildings.

As with all entertainment offered at the seaside, the gardens were a commercial venture. When the Saltburn Improvement Company met in February 1861 they offered a Mr Bowker £10 to design some ornamental gardens to be sited in the Glen. When the board reconvened in January 1862 Mr Bowker tendered his plan whose centrepiece was an Italian Garden, the remainder of the Glen to be laid out with a pattern of zig-zag walks interspersed with open green spaces. Financial considerations reduced the scale of the project, but by February a Mr Everatt was employed as Head Gardener at a wage of 18/- (90p) a week. While he began to supervise the landscaping, a lodge was built (bearing the date 1862 over the door) half way down Camp Bank, backed by a series of greenhouses almost down to Skelton Beck.

Bore holes were also sunk in Camp Bank and a sample of mineral water was analysed in Liverpool. The directors were pleased when the report dated 25 August 1864 stated the mineral water was comparable to that of Harrogate. It was hoped to develop Saltburn as a spa town, attracting the rich and famous. The spring was rerouted and a stone fountain erected, complete with metal drinking cups. Although the water became popular

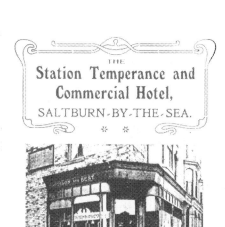

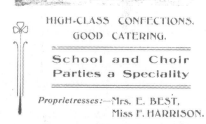

Opposite: The Italian garden, showing the rear of the gardener's cottage built 1862 at top right.

55

with locals, the anticipated crowds did not flock to cure their ailments.

The Rev J.C. Atkinson wrote of the gardens:'...*the result is certainly striking and beautiful in no ordinary degree. Croquet lawns, Italian gardening, Spa fountains, greenhouses and their contents, and finally the hanging-woods in the higher part of the ravine all unite to lend a charm which only a personal visit can realise.*' He placed them *'second to scarcely any in the kingdom.'*

Admission to the gardens was gained via any of three turnstiles; one opposite the Zetland, one by the gardener's lodge and one near the beach by the beck. Residents, however, could buy season tickets. During their life as a business venture, the owners made sure the gardens attracted customers. In the same newspaper edition that carried Lillie Langtree advertising Pear's soap alongside a report on Oscar Wilde's lecture in Middlesbrough, it was stated the subscriptions for the Saltburn band were £417 for 1883 season. This band would alternate, playing on the pier in the morning then in the gardens on the afternoon. Singing contests were regularly held as well as Rechabite galas, Methodist outings, Wesleyan fetes and gatherings of the Ancient Order of Shepherds. Importantly, one great success was the installation of electric lighting in 1887 to provide illuminations, 13 years before the townsfolk had the choice of replacing gas lighting in their homes. Incidentally, the author met someone who bought a house in Eden Street as recently as 1976/77 and found to his amazement there was no electricity, only gas mantles!

Right: The gardener's cottage.

Centre: Thomas Metcalfe, head gardener for 40 years from 1899, among his beloved dalias.

Far Right: The Albert Temple, originally the portico of Barnard Castle railway station, erected at Saltburn in 1867 as a memorial to Prince Albert, the Queen's consort who died in 1861.

Firework displays by Brocks of Crystal Palace were a regular feature at the opening of the season. The gardens would be filled with couples strolling at dusk, rockets and catharine wheels drawing gasps of delight. When the last burst of colour died away the fairy lights would be switched on, bedecking the bandstand and strung between the trees. Nightlights in glass globes also added to the effect.

The gardens retained their appeal through the turn of the century but in 1901 when they were opened free to the public, seats and trees were damaged by vandals. Entrance fees were re-introduced, free access only allowed to locals out of season. The Glen may have tamed by the hand of man but nature still lurked in the undergrowth. During the first week of November 1903 a 22 inch long Adder was killed along the Rosewalk. As late as 1900 at Marske Mill dam boys could be seen spearing salmon swimming up Skelton Beck to spawn. Rabbits have always been numerous, and where they roam foxes follow. Squirrels too are common.

While the Owners of the Middlesbrough Estate have retained some property in Saltburn, the gardens were sold to the Urban District Council in 1936 for an undisclosed sum after a special act of parliament was obtained. Some of the features like shelters and the graceful span of the Ha'penny bridge have disappeared, but the Italian garden still retains its oval shape. Each year a riot of colour pleases those visitors who relax on the seats round the flower beds.

Opposite: The bandstand in the Pleasure Grounds where performances were given on summer afternoons. Bombed during World War II, debris was scattered high up the opposite hillside. A flowerbed is now on this site.

Hazelgrove

Although Saltburn's beach was available to all, there was no free green park. It had long stuck in residents' craws that they had to buy tickets in order to enjoy their town's woods and gardens. When control was finally wrested from the Improvement Company by the Local Board of Health in 1880, it was at last felt the residents, rather than the owners' wishes would be served.

Not until 1896 did the park question arise, shortly after the Local Board was superceded by the Urban District Council. The following year an estimate placed the cost of a park at nearly £2,000, a sum the council lacked. In 1899, however, Lord Zetland offered 8 acres in Hazelgrove as a free gift provided no building would ever be allowed. The council accepted, then changed their minds, perhaps influenced by the projected £892 cost of providing drainage. The townspeople successfully fought their councillors, and when a ballot was held, 76% of the votes were in favour of the park. Eventually in 1904 Hazelgrove was open for recreation.

Below opposite: Hazelgrove looking toward the sea c1920.

Above opposite: Looking inland at Hazelgrove's west side.

A Man Of All Trades

The motto over his newspaper's banner read *Open to all, servile to none*. This also appears to have been William Rapp's personal philosophy. He was open to all ideas, both in serving the community and also providing a living for himself and his family. Along with his sons in premises at 3, Dundas Street (now the Victoria) he stretched out tentacles in all directions. Posterity will remember him best perhaps as publisher of the *Saltburn Times*, the *Saltburn & Guisbro' Times* and the *Saltburn & Loftus Advertiser* (the latter in partnership with a Loftus businessman). While his printing works produced the newspapers he also published guides and at least one book (a second edition of Blakeborough). His shop advertised a subscription library of 5,000 volumes, also selling all manner of stationery and fancy goods. In addition he acted as an estate agent and held the important appointment of Postmaster to Saltburn. He found time to be auditor of the Pier Company, Vice-President of the Saltburn, Skelton & Loftus District Building Society while serving as parishoners warden. William Rapp was a man who squeezed a lot into his life.

At Your Service!

INTENDING VISITORS to Saltburn, on communicating with

W. Rapp & Sons, Ltd.

House and Estate Agents,

Will find that only the **BEST FURNISHED HOUSES AND RELIABLE APARTMENTS** are recommended, and no charge is made for securing Visitors' requirements.

Upon application they will be pleased to send suitable recommendations by return.

Having been established in the town over 40 years, W. R. & S., Ltd., have that personal knowledge of both people and houses which enable them to make recommendations with confidence. W. R. & S., Ltd., have found accommodation for all classes including the Nobility and Cabinet Ministers, and have been encouraged by the appreciation which has been tendered to them unsolicited.

There premises are quite near the station and W. R. & S., Ltd., take a pleasure in helping Visitors to enjoy their sojourn at this choicest of watering places.

W. RAPP & SONS, Ltd.,

THE SALTBURN LIBRARY

(5,000 VOLUMES)

Office of Saltburn Guides and Visitors' List.

SALTBURN-BY-THE-SEA

Mr. T. C. TOMKINS

WILL

SELL BY AUCTION,

ABSOLUTELY WITHOUT RESERVE,

Under power of a Bill of Sale, registered April 27th, 1874,

On WEDNESDAY, JAN. 20, 1875,

THE HOUSEHOLD

FURNITURE

AND EFFECTS,

LATE THE PROPERTY OF MISS E. TROUSDALE,

Consisting of Drawing Room Suite, upholstered in Green Repp; Centre Table, several Iron Bedsteads, Feather Beds, Chairs, Tables, School Desks, Drawing Boards, Chests of Drawers, Wardrobe, and a large quantity of Effects which have been removed to the

SALE ROOM IN AMBER STREET.

May be viewed Tuesday, January 19th, 1875, and Morning of Sale.

Owing to the large Number of Lots, the Sale will commence at 11 a.m.

RAPP, MACHINE PRINTER, SALTBURN-BY-THE-SEA.

SALTBURN-BY-THE-SEA.

RAILWAY JUBILEE.

THE BAND

OF HER MAJESTY'S

GRENADIER

GUARDS,

Under the direction of Mr. Dan Godfrey,

WILL PERFORM ON

TUESDAY, SEPTEMBER 28TH,

IN THE

Private Grounds of the Improvement Company, from 1 p.m. to 3 p.m.

ADMISSION SIXPENCE.

A. B. MOSS PRINTER, SALTBURN-BY-THE-SEA.

Lovely Saltburn-by-the-Sea

Previous page: Two contemporary posters. W. Rapp fell ill in 1875 and sold the business but rebought it a year later.
Opposite: A view from the railway bridge at the junction of Marske Mill Lane (now Guisborough Road). On the left is Zetland Terrace, while the west end of Oxford Street can be seen on the right. Princes Road and the Crescent now cover the land to the right of the railway lines.

Numerous visitors brought prosperity to the town, enabling growth inland and westward. With no television or radio to go home to, the thousands who arrived by train on cheap excursion tickets stayed until late evening. At the dawn of the 20th century a typical day at the seaside would begin when the children raced from the station to the beach. When buckets and spades became gritty with sand, there were donkey rides or a walk along the pier where parents could listen to the band. Perhaps mother and father wished to swim in the sea. A bathing machine could be hired from Mr Woodrow who would tow it by horse into the rippling breakers. They could change inside then enter the sea almost in privacy. Not together, of course. It was July 1902 before the council allowed mixed bathing, stipulating machines had to be used between Hazelgrove and Skelton Beck, offenders

1899

J. T. WOODROW,
1, PRIMROSE TERRACE,
SALTBURN-BY-THE-SEA,
YORKSHIRE.

Above: An advert for Woodrow's bathing machines. The family also had a coal business.
Opposite: The seafront lined with bathing machines, by the 1920's unused.

liable to a £2 fine. A boatman was provided should anyone get out of their depth.

After a picnic lunch washed down by a flask of tea from one of the seafront stalls, the sideshows at Cat Nab pleasure ground would prove tempting during the afternoon. Ice creams and rides on the boatswings before buying a ticket through the iron turnstile to the ornamental gardens. With the trellis-like span of the Ha'penny bridge high overhead, a slow stroll ended at the Italian garden. The elaborate tower and chimneys of Rushpool Hall could be seen above the trees. Teas were served in the gardens while music drifted from the bandstand, spectators gathered on the terraces cut into the bankside above (see page 61).

For those still with energy, a gate by the gardener's lodge led into Riftswood. Below the Glenside path the beck carved a passage between rockwalls known as the 'hanging woods'. The path eventually joined Marske Mill Lane where it swooped down to the farm (see pages 51/53) then along below the arches of Skelton viaduct to the mill dam.

Up in the town, the afternoon brought 'teaser' performances by pierrots to advertise their early evening shows. Several troupes vied for custom. One pitch was on the lower promenade west of the peir, another on the sands to the east, while a third was opposite the New Marine Hotel. The early pitches of raised boards later evolved into proper stages with canvas roofs, scenery, with bathing tents or caravans used as dressing rooms. These performers were really licensed buskers, paying Saltburn Council a fee which

Left: Davis' White Coons.
Above: Pierrots performing on the lower promenade c1920.
Opposite: A captivating postcard sent from Saltburn.

entitled them to pass a hat round the audience. In return they danced, sang, played musical instruments, told funny stories, recited monologues and acted sketches. Nowadays, jaded by slick televised entertainment (all gaffes skillfully edited out) it is easy to regard the pierrots as amateurish, but they returned year after year, collecting enough to make a living. *Grapho's Jovial Jollies* played at least 15 seasons at Saltburn between wars. During World War 1 their talent earned them a run of 16 weeks at Crewe New Theatre. Many English artistes 'backed up' for part or all of their acts, following the example of popular negro entertainers. This is reflected in stage-names like *Little Tommy's Nigger Troupe* and *George Davis' White Coons*, both of whom were well received at Saltburn along with Scarborough's Catlins.

The troupes must have rehearsed extensive repertoires as visitors probably watched several performances, assuming they could rally enough coins to chink in the hat! One of these pierrot shows would round off the day, weary children protesting as they were shepherded to the inclined tramway, squeezing one last moment of pleasure from the view of the pier as they rode up the cliff. After a wait under the glass roof of the railway station, the steam engine would huff and puff through the fields back to the industrial heartland of Cleveland. The discomfort of sand stuck between toes and the smell of damp towels would be forgotten as urchins curled up to fall asleep on the carriage seats. Parents would glance at each other and smile.

All in all, it had been a long day.

I AM FAIRLY CARRIED AWAY WITH THE BEAUTY OF Saltburn

The Fair, Saltburn

Looking To The Future

The opinion has been forwarded the resort's decline is due to cheap holidays abroad. Remember that during Saltburn's halcyon days the average working man did not have paid holidays; the town was sustained by an influx of day-trippers. In fact, today Saltburn is *more* accessible as most people have the convenience of cars. That the town still draws visitors can be seen on any sunny day when it becomes almost impossible to find a parking space.

The problem is the glamour of Saltburn has evaporated. A day at the seaside requires more than just a beach; as modern museums need more than an endless array of glass cases. It is presentation that is important. If it is Saltburn's character that is appealing, then that character should be enhanced. If the Saltburn of the future is not to be a sprawl of mismatched buildings with no overall personality, then strict planning guidelines should be laid down so potential investors will be aware what style and building materials are acceptable. The seafront especially requires careful restoration and a creative eye to blend the new successfully with the old.

Then perhaps those that remember will not gaze wistfully at the photographs in this book and recall: 'Ah, but Saltburn *was* Saltburn *in those days.'*

Opposite: A busy day, probably Whit Monday. On the right can be seen the turnstile to the Pleasure Grounds, then beyond, a steam driven roundabout and side stalls round to the bathing machines.

The Author

Chris Scott Wilson was born in Middlesbrough and was educated at Barnard Castle School and West Middlesbrough College of Further Education. He has worked in the hotel trade, a newspaper office, accountancy, non-destructive testing, the entertainment industry and has held various jobs within British Steel, currently working on the Redcar complex as a Sampling Technician Supervisor. In addition to the books listed in the front of this publication, he has contributed to *Dalesman* magazine, *The Yorkshire Annual,* the late *Cleveland Courier,* the *Cleveland Clarion* and Middlesbrough's *Evening Gazette.* Presently working on another book, he lives with his wife Susan in Saltburn By Sea.